PBD

Dear Parents,

Talking to your children about their experiences in life and the lessons they can learn is so important. My goal in sharing my stories and Life Lessons is to give you a fun and playful way to guide the conversation. For more information, go to my website at **www.meetmardi.com**.

With much love,

Mardi

www.mascotbooks.com

Meet Mardi: Mardi's New Home

For more information, please contact:

Mascot Books
560 Herndon Parkway #120
Herndon, VA 20170
info@mascotbooks.com

Library of Congress Control Number: 2016901670

CPSIA Code: PRT0416
ISBN: 978-1-63177-442-3

Printed in the United States

Meet Mardi

Mardi's New Home

by Linda Dembo

art by Romney Vasquez

Smack, stick, slap! went the sandals against the floor. The small puppy chased the feet as they raced past her crate. She had to move quickly. The lady of the house was fast.

The smallest puppy, or Puppy Number Four, as the lady called her, wagged her tail. "Yip, Yap!" her brothers and sisters exclaimed. Now it was time to play!

Once outside, the smallest puppy hid until her sister wandered by. "Bow, wow, wow!" the little puppy yelled.

"Yip!" shouted her sister. Then the chase began. The tiny puppy loved playing with her sister best.

The smallest puppy also loved making new discoveries. One day, she saw a blue creature land in the grass. She walked up until it took off. *Whoosh!* Into the sky it soared. The little puppy ran underneath it. She ran as far as she could until it went into the clouds. That was fun!

Another time, the smallest puppy saw a furry creature. She chased it until it began chasing her. Yikes! Fortunately, her sister scared it away. "Meow!" it screeched. That was scary but also fun!

At night, the puppies talked themselves to sleep while watching the stars in the dark Louisiana night sky.

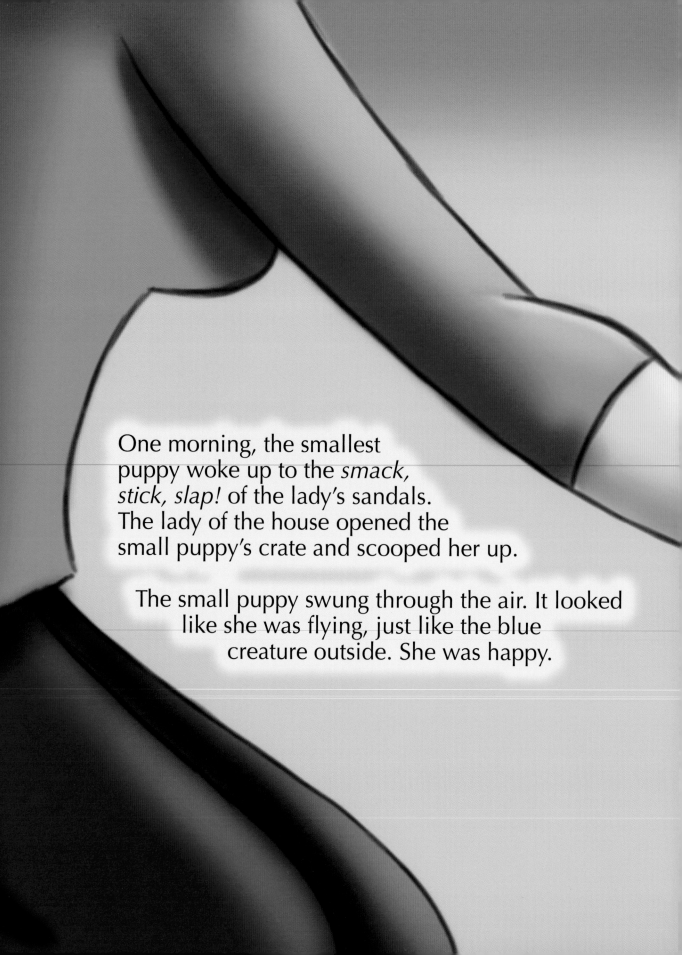

One morning, the smallest
puppy woke up to the *smack,*
stick, slap! of the lady's sandals.
The lady of the house opened the
small puppy's crate and scooped her up.

The small puppy swung through the air. It looked
like she was flying, just like the blue
creature outside. She was happy.

Plop! She landed in a man's arms. "Good news, Edgar! The little apricot-colored puppy was sold," the lady shouted. "Get Puppy Number Four ready for the next flight."

The man carried the small puppy out the door. She scrambled in his arms to look behind him. She saw her brothers and sister and then the door closed.

The small puppy was put in a dark room. She was scared and shaking. Then, she felt the entire room shake. They were moving!

"Yelp!" she exclaimed. Even though she was scared, the small puppy stood up and barked loudly, "Bow, wow, wow!"

A big dog stood up in his crate. He saw the puppy and thought of his friend back home. His friend would jump over the fence and play chase all day! He was really going to miss him.

When they landed, the small puppy was carried away. She saw people standing as her crate moved past them. Then, a lady ran up to the little puppy.

The tiny puppy heard, "For Linda in California. Puppy Number Four, from the puppy house in Louisiana." The small puppy once again was scooped up in the air.

She came face to face with a lady who said, "Hi! My name is Linda. I've been waiting for you."

Linda looked around at all the people who got off the Louisiana flight. They wore Mardi Gras t-shirts. She smiled.

"Hi…Mardi? Does that name work for you?" Mardi wagged her tail and licked Linda's nose. Now, Mardi had a new name and a new home.

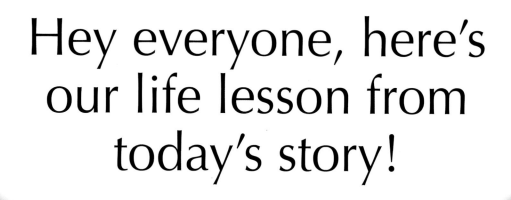

Hey everyone, here's our life lesson from today's story!

One day Mardi is running around as Puppy Number Four, playing with her brothers and sisters in Louisiana. The next day, she is getting off an airplane, meeting Linda, getting her forever name, Mardi, and giving big kisses to her new mom.

What does Mardi's adventure teach us?

Lesson #1

- Life changes can be good. We may get scared, but things can always wind up with a…lick on the nose!

About the Author

Linda Dembo is a children's author dedicated to telling stories that focus on the goodness in everybody. Originally from the Midwest, she now lives in beautiful Southern California with her husband and the newest member of their family, Mardi.

About Mardi

Mardi is a smart, friendly, and amazingly kind apricot Shih Tzu-Poodle. She was born in Louisiana during the festival of Mardi Gras, 2012. Then she boarded an airplane and began her new life with her new family.

Today, Mardi works as a therapy dog, helping patients at a local hospital feel happy as they go through their medical procedures. Mardi has many friends and loves meeting new people...and of course, new dogs!